ETERNAL RIDE

Hellions Motorcycle Club

CHELSEA CAMARON

D1714337

ETERNAL RIDE

A Hellions Ride Novella

HELL RAISERS DEMANDING EXTREME CHAOS

USA TODAY BESTSELLING AUTHOR

Chelsea Camaron

ETERNAL RIDE

Eternal Ride

Ride for life.

Two people once lost.

Two people once broken.

Two people who have endured the pain.

One love brought them together. One love healed their hearts and made them whole again. One love carries them through the good times and the bad.

Shooter and Tessie have faced the shadows and demons that haunted them. They have built their life together on a solid foundation of love, friendship, and understanding.

The only thing they haven't done is make it official.

Join them and the entire Hellions motorcycle club

family as they commit their love for the eternal ride together.

Series Reading Order:

One Ride

Forever Ride

Merciless Ride

Eternal Ride

Innocent Ride

Simple Ride

Heated Ride

Ride with Me (Hellions MC and Ravage MC Duel) co-written with Ryan Michele

Originals Ride

Final Ride

CONTENT WARNING

Intended for mature audiences only

This series contains strong language, strong sexual situations, and violence. Please do not buy if any of this offends you.

This is not meant to be a true or exact depiction of a motorcycle club, rather a work of fiction meant to entertain.

ONE

SIMPLE

SHOOTER

"Are you sure I shouldn't at least go back to work at Brinkley's?" Tessie asks in all sincerity.

Sincere or not, I look over to her from our kitchen table as if she has two heads. It is the same fight we have month after month.

After she agreed to move in with me, she took time off to help her mom adjust and be at home more for Axel. Brinkley's has told her she can come back to work anytime, but that is a decision I leave solely up to her.

"Baby, come here."

She walks over slowly. When she is close enough, I reach out and pull her to my lap.

"Why do we keep having this conversation?"

"I don't know," she whispers. "Maybe because I'm stubborn." She bites at her bottom lip, making my dick twitch in my jeans. God, she is even sexy in sweats and an old tank top. The littlest things turn me on with this woman. Hell, if I am honest, everything about her turns me on.

"You wanna work, then work. You wanna stay home with your mom and Axel, stay home. Baby, you're on the bank account; you see the statements. We aren't rich, but we damn sure don't struggle."

"That's your money, Shooter," she states calmly, just like she does every time we discuss money.

My anger rises yet again over this same topic.

"Tessie, is that my ring on your finger?"

"Yes," she answers, looking down at her left hand.

"Is it my last name you will soon have?"

"Yes, Shooter." She blows out a frustrated breath.

"Am I a man?"

"Andy," she chastises my smartass remark.

"Baby, am I a man?" She nods at me. "Am I your man?"

"Yes, Shooter, you know all this."

"Then tell me, why is it such a problem for me as a man to take care of you as my woman? To take care of my family? Are we not building something to be a family?" I watch her, trying to gauge where her head is.

"Yes, Shooter. It's just hard. I'm so used to doing it all. It's hard to accept help."

Jumping up from my chair, I stand her on her feet.

"Help!" I roar at her. She flinches, not used to me getting so worked up. "Fuck, Tessie! This isn't help. This is us being together. Dammit, I take care of what's mine. Last I checked, you are fuckin' mine. Unless something's changed that you need to tell me about ..."

Without a word, she rolls up on her tiptoes and kisses me. My frustration only adds to the passion as I suck hard on her bottom lip before pulling away, releasing her mouth with a pop.

"Baby, if you need to work, then work. But, please, stop the shit over money. I get it, baby, I really do. Don't call what I do help, ever. It's not help; it's being a man."

"Okay, Shooter."

"Okay, Shooter? That was a little too easy." I raise an eyebrow at her.

"I am yours, and you're the type of man to take care of what's yours. So I need to decide if I want to work for me and not about the money."

"You gonna marry me sometime soon, then?" If she

is going to concede so easily over the money, then now is the time to push my luck on the other topic we have not quite been seeing eye-to-eye on.

The wedding. The wedding that I want to happen, like yesterday. Although the road to get us here was far from easy, I have never wanted something so much in my life—to have her carry my last name, to have her carry my babies, and most importantly, to have her share my life for always.

"Shooter," she whines, knowing this is yet another topic we will go in circles over.

"What? I want you to have my name, have my babies, and sooner rather than later. Just sayin'." I try to look innocent, but I seriously doubt she finds any of this innocent on my end.

"So, take me to the court house. I told you this already."

Exasperating woman.

"We are not getting married at the damn court house. First, I tend to avoid court houses. I don't know any Hellion that will willingly go to one. Nor do I want one of the happiest days of our lives to be at a court house. That doesn't work for me, Tessie. Second, your mom had one daughter. Baby, little girls dream of the dress, the man, the day, and so do their moms. What's the problem with you having all that?"

She sighs. "Shooter, weddings are expensive."

"Fuckin' money. Why does everything come back to money, Tessie? I may not be rich, but damn, I'm not poor."

She reaches up, placing her hands on my chest. "Shooter, this isn't about your money. I know you provide well for us. I know you want to give me the wedding of my dreams. It honestly has nothing to do with you. It's me, Shooter. I can't see spending some crazy amount of money on one day, even if it is the biggest day of my life outside of having Axel."

Tears pool in her eyes. God, I hate when she cries.

"There was a time not so long ago when I counted pennies just to get by. There was a time when, yes, I went to the grocery store to use the coin machine just to be able to get milk and cereal for Axel." As the tears fall, I reach up and run my thumbs under her eyes to wipe them away. "I can't forget my struggles, Shooter. You make everything feel so easy it scares me sometimes. You take care of me in a way I've never been taken care of before. Even when I was a kid with Momma, we struggled. I've never known how to relax and not worry about having enough to get by until my next night with good tips or my next paycheck."

"What can we do so we aren't at the court house, but you don't feel like you're breaking the bank? Tell me what you want."

"I want memories. I want family, friends, you, me,

and Axel to have this together. I don't want a church. I don't want some big shindig. I just want simple."

"Baby, if it's memories you want, it's memories you'll get."

TWO

MIAMI

SHOOTER

Sun, surf, and sand. Never would I have imagined Brett 'Ice' Grady coming to Miami and settling down. Things aren't always what they seem, I guess.

There is an anxiousness inside me as we make the drive southbound.

Tessie is cute when she gets all nervous about meeting someone close to me. She has talked to Ice and Brooke here and there on the phone calls we have managed, but the whole meeting them is different. Hell,

I thought she was going to cry when she met Fred, Tracie's dad, for the first time. My woman feels deeply, loves harder, and takes on everything for everyone. She has brought Fred into our little family as if he is one of our own. He lost his wife and daughter, but he still has me, my girl, and our boy.

Axel spends time out at the garage with me, learning everything from the man who taught me when I wasn't that much older than he is now. Life is good for a change, for all of us.

Since the day we got the graduation announcement in the mail from Brooke, Tessie has been a little on edge. She fires away question after question daily about Ice and the rest of the guys. All of it takes me back.

Throughout the years, we have done the best we could with our situations. I will never forget watching Ice hit his knees when our command gave him the news of Erin's accident and death. He went home, sorted his shit, and carried on, even though he has never been the same. Then, when Tracie killed herself, he left little Brooke with his mom to help me sort my shit and try to figure out how to carry on.

Over the years, we have kept in touch, and I have always been around to watch Brooke's milestones. Time is passing by so quickly. It seems as if it was just yesterday we were trying to make it home in time for her kindergarten graduation. Yes, Brooke had eight Army Green Berets all side-by-side at her kindergarten graduation, watching her pig-tailed little ass get a blank piece of rolled up paper while wearing the tiniest cap and gown ever. While she smiled brightly at us, we all proudly smiled right back alongside Ice's mom.

That little girl captured all of us, and now I get to make the drive to be there to watch her wear a grown up sized cap and gown, once again walking across a stage for a rolled up piece of paper. Only when she smiles down at us this time, her grandmother won't be there as her mother wasn't there the first time. My chest tightens thinking of how things have changed over the years.

Looking in the rearview mirror, I watch Axel as he plays some game on his tablet. What will it feel like the day he graduates? He is as much mine as he is Rex's son. Speaking of which, things are good for us now. He understands why Tessie didn't tell him and why I kept her secret, as well. Still, it is not my proudest moment, but I will always have Tessie's back through anything.

We have found a routine that works and have become a family unit of our own. Rex sees Axel when he is in town. We do stuff all together, and he keeps him on his own, as well. We spend important moments and holidays together so no one feels left out. That way, Axel truly gets everyone he is close to, all in one place.

How will my brother-in-arms react to my son? Hell, how will he react to my fiancée? Ice knows I have an ol' lady and a son, but we haven't had time to catch each other up with all the details of the changes I have had.

Pulling into the parking garage of the hotel we are staying at, I smile as I think about how good my life really is now. As I look beside me at Tessie's beautiful face, I feel complete. No longer am I a lost man rambling through life with no purpose. I am now taking every breath to have more moments with her.

Once we are unpacked, we go out to dinner downtown. This is a reminder of why I have zero desire to live in the city. Hell, I thought Charlotte was a pain in the ass to drive around when I make the commute to work. Home has nothing on South Beach.

Tessie pokes around her plate. "Brooke and I get along on the phone, but meeting all of them at once… It's overwhelming. Do you think they'll like me?"

"Baby, are you seriously asking me this?"

"Yeah, Shooter. These guys are important to you. I want to make a good impression."

I smile at her. "You and Axel are more important. I don't give a shit what anyone thinks of you. It doesn't change a damn thing between us."

"I love you, Andy." She looks at me before finally eating.

"Love you, baby, for eternity."

"Enough with the mushy talk, you two. Young ears are here, ya know," Axel pipes in.

I reach over and ruffle his hair.

My chest tightens looking at my woman and my son. It doesn't get much better than this right here.

CHAPTER
THREE

EYES WIDE OPEN

SHOOTER

"Ice!" I call out once I spot my brother-in-arms. We have just arrived and gotten out of the car with our graduation tickets. To need to have a ticket to enter into a high school graduation seems crazy, but I guess, with a school so large, they have to limit the guests in attendance.

Both Ice and his daughter look over and then Brooke screams, "Uncle Shooter," and takes off running at me.

Ice comes over, holding the hand of a brunette woman I have never seen before. Another teen who looks related to the brunette follows closely behind. They must be his woman Morgan and her sister Madyson. Brooke has given me updates, but we have all been so busy that it wasn't a complete catch up. Plus, love the girl, but she talks a lot. I can't help getting lost in my own thoughts as I listen to the rambling teen.

After Ice greets me in our usual man half-hug, back slap thing, I smile at the woman beside him.

"Shooter, this is Morgan," Ice officially introduces us.

"Damn, never thought I'd see the day someone melted that permafrost around your heart. Congrats, asshole," I joke while extending my hand to her.

She gives my hand a quick, friendly shake before stepping back next to Ice. I give her a knowing smile. He has her trained already. Yes, no one touches what belongs to Ice. Can't say I blame him, though; beyond a handshake, if anyone touches Tessie, my inner cave man goes ape-shit crazy.

"Fuck you!" Ice replies in jest at my smirk while wrapping his arm around Morgan's shoulders to let her know she is back where she belongs.

I step back and wrap my arm around Tessie. Time for introductions of my own. "Brooke, Ice, this is my ol' lady Tessie and our boy Axel."

"Nice to meet you in person after talking on the phone so much." Brooke bounces excitedly.

"I can't believe you're actually here, Uncle Shooter," Brooke continues with a smile that lights up the world.

"Wouldn't miss it for the world, baby girl."

"She's got the ring, so when are you givin' her the name?" Ice asks me bluntly, nodding at Tessie's left hand.

"As soon as she gives me a day and time to show up," I proudly respond, wishing I had a definite answer or, better yet, had this already done. Nodding to Morgan, I reply, "You better move that one in before someone else swoops in and snatches that prize right out of your hands." I give her a playful wink. Anything to get the topic changed from my non-impending nuptials.

"Just needed to get these two graduated. After today, that's a definite, brother."

Watching Morgan, she apparently isn't aware of my brother's plans for them. Her jaw drops open in surprise for a split second.

"Excuse me. I'm not moving in with you." Her challenging him almost makes me want to laugh.

"Why the fuck not?" Ice asks as Madyson and Brooke start to laugh behind them.

"You haven't even managed to tell me you love me, and we've been together for over a year; why in the hell would I move in with you?"

Oh, hell.

His entire demeanor changes from one of joking to complete seriousness. He turns to Morgan, cupping her face in both of his hands, forcing her to meet his stare. "I'm a man of actions because they speak louder than words. Sweetheart, you want the words, you need the words, you got them. I told you, once I see something I want, I don't let it go. Morgan, I love you. I love you yesterday, I love you today, I love you tomorrow, and I will love you for the rest of my days."

I feel like I am intruding on something I shouldn't, yet it's beautiful in its own way. Watching my brother have this, knowing everything he has been through, my chest fills with more emotion than I ever thought possible.

With that seemingly settled, we head inside to attend the graduation ceremony. Squeezing Tessie's hand, I am in awe of the woman beside me and all she has been through. I never thought I could feel this much emotion for one person. I would walk through Hell and back to give this woman every dream she has ever had.

The ceremony goes on for a while before the students are each called across the stage. Proudly, I watch the once little girl who has grown into one of the strongest young women I know accept her diploma. Life hasn't been fair or easy for Brooke or Ice, but they have endured.

After making plans to meet at Ice's house for a cookout, we go back to the hotel to change clothes.

"Baby, you okay?" I question. Tessie has been extremely quiet since meeting everyone.

She eyes me cautiously. "What about here?"

"Ummm … clue me in a little more as to what you are asking for, and I promise I'll do my best." I am not following where she is going with this conversation. She is tense, and I don't fucking like it one bit.

Her chest rises and falls more quickly, letting me know she is getting worked up over whatever is on her mind. I move over to her and put my hands on her biceps, just to touch her as I focus on her demeanor.

"Breathe, baby. Inhale. Tell me what you want. Exhale."

"Could we get married here?" she whispers, looking me directly in the eye.

"You really gotta ask me that? Of course we can."

She bites her bottom lip as she looks sideways to Axel jumping on the hotel bed. "Can you get my mom here? I know I'm asking for a lot. If you would rather wait until we're home, that's fine. It's just—"

"It's just nothing. You want it, you got it, baby. I'll have Rex get on a plane with your mom and get her here." I smile at her before I crash my lips down on hers.

"Ewwww … .Shooter, girls have cooties, even

moms sometimes," Axel attempts to interrupt, but I don't stop kissing her. She is making me the happiest man on the planet right now, so no, I am not going to stop kissing her until I am damn good and ready, kid or no kid. "Usually, it works. I'm losing my touch," Axel mutters to himself before turning his attention elsewhere as his mom laughs uncontrollably in my arms, breaking our kiss.

God, I love the little fucker.

Looking down at the woman who owns my heart and soul completely, I can't believe she really is ready.

"You sure, baby? Don't feel pressured into anything."

"Seeing Ice and Morgan have their moment earlier, it opened my eyes—actions speak louder than words. I don't want to spend more time treading water. I want nothing more in this life than to be your wife, so why wait? I want this, you want this, and besides, what's simpler than a beach wedding?"

Kissing her breathless again, I can't help feeling complete every time she is in my arms.

"Here we go again," Axel mutters on a sigh.

Son, if you only knew what I would be doing to your momma if you weren't in here right now.

FOUR

CHAPTER FOUR

GIRL TALK

Whew. I am going to do this. I am really going to marry Shooter. He called Rex, and my mom will be here tomorrow morning with him. At sunset, I will commit the rest of my days to the man who literally brought me out of the darkest of times.

Arriving at Ice's house, I am overwhelmed at the size. Never would I have pictured the club President of the Regulators MC to reside in a gated community. His house would swallow ours completely, with room to spare. What are those guys in cuts doing to make this kind of money?

"Things aren't always what they seem, baby. He makes sure his girl stays safe," Shooter states, reading my mind. Knowing first-hand the dangers of a rival club —or hell, even a so-called affiliate—no one can be too safe in this lifestyle.

"Well, in a place like this, I would think she is safe, as long as she doesn't get lost."

Shooter laughs at me, causing my heart rate to pick up. Every part of me is connected to this man.

"Come on, baby. Don't be intimidated. Ice and his crew are good guys." He is looking at me intently, worried for me. Honestly, I don't like crowds. I am far from comfortable around bikers that aren't Hellions. With Shooter by my side, I can face anything, though, including a strange club.

"I'm okay." I smile over at him.

"We don't have to be here. We have a big day of our own coming up. I can call Ice and explain."

"I'm good, honey. I want to hang out with your friends."

With a quick kiss, he gets out of the vehicle, opening the door for Axel before making his way around to my door. As I climb out, he squeezes my hand reassuringly. This man always has my back.

Making our way through the house, we get to the backyard where the party is in full swing. Bikers abound, beer drinking brothers stand with their old ladies at their sides, and their kids run around like they are at the park.

When I see a cut that doesn't match the patches of the Regulators, my heart skips a beat. I still struggle with what happened to me. Seeing colors I am not used to puts me on edge, waiting for a Desert Ghost to show up.

Seeing the cut of the Savage Outlaws, I blow out a breath. On his side is a signature knife Shooter has told me all about. When I look up to the face of the man, I see it is indeed Bowie, with who I assume is his ol' lady Shay at his side. I thought I saw him briefly with Lock at the graduation ceremony, but it was so crowded I couldn't take everyone in. Having served in the Army with Shooter and Ice, I have seen pictures of him with the team from their missions in different parts of the world. He doesn't look exactly the same, but the features are similar enough to discern who is who.

After a quick chin lift in greeting, Shooter guides us over to where Ice is standing with Morgan tucked into his side. They again do their man hug, back slap thing that I will never understand before we step back to chat.

"Can I go play horseshoes with everyone, Momma?" Axel asks.

"Sure thing, buddy. Stay where you can see us, though." I send him off to be a kid. Letting go is hard to do.

"Have you set a date yet?" Morgan asks me in what I think is her attempt at casual conversation.

Proudly, Shooter pipes up, "Tomorrow at sunset."

"Look at you. Smug bastard," Ice replies at Shooter's puffing of his chest when he made our announcement.

"I'm hoping you and all the boys will be there," Shooter adds, still smiling.

"Always, brother."

"Oh. My. God," Morgan emphasizes.

"Sweetheart, that shit is for the bedroom, not with our friends," Ice chimes in playfully.

Suddenly, Morgan grabs me by the wrist, taking me with her towards the house. "We have to find something for me and the girls to wear."

"Brooke is ruining you!" Ice calls out as his woman keeps dragging me.

When I give Shooter a look, pleading with him to save me, he only shrugs his shoulders and mouths, 'sorry'.

Once inside what I assume to be Brooke's room, I can't help laughing as Morgan looks in the teen's closet.

"Dammit. All her clothes will get me in trouble. Wait, maybe I want to be in trouble," she mutters to herself. She stops and brings her finger up to tap on her jaw as she contemplates whether she wants to be 'punished' or not.

"Anticipation makes it hotter," I add, letting her know my mind is just as dirty and so is my man.

We both fall into a fit of giggles. It is an odd thing for me. Since Shooter has come into my life, I laugh, I relax, and I breathe.

"Does it ever dull out?" she suddenly asks me seriously.

"What do you mean?"

"I don't know. Forget it," she backtracks.

"We ol' ladies have to stick together. I know we don't know each other well, but I would like to change that," I state honestly. I don't have many friends. If I am real with myself, I don't have friends outside of the Hellions. Not that it is a problem, but Morgan seems nice enough.

"How long have you been with a biker? The sex with Ice is ah-maz-ing; I just wonder if it dulls out."

"Hell no, it never dulls out."

"How long have you and Shooter been together? Casey, my best friend, she says the sex is hot because bikers are hot. She has been with regular guys, and she says it's not the same." She looks at me nervously. "I've only ever been with Ice. Don't get me wrong, he seems happy with umm … what we do, ya know, but does it ever waver? The last year has been the best of my life, but I feel like I'm waiting for the other shoe to drop sometimes."

"Shooter and I have this long history together." For some reason, something in me changes with Morgan, and I share with her something I don't talk about much these days. "He saved me. I was being attacked." I shift on my feet uncomfortably. How will she take my story? "I was violated. It could have been worse, but Shooter, he saved me. He is my rock. I don't have a ton of experience, but what I have with Shooter is off-the-charts amazing." I giggle nervously as she looks at me somberly.

"How did you overcome that?"

"Time, patience, love, understanding, and Shooter. He saved me from myself."

Tears fill her eyes. "My sister … she was… umm … kidnapped. Things happened. She is doing better, but I worry that she will never feel normal again."

"You want me to be honest with you?" She nods her head. "What is normal? You were a virgin until Ice. You have great sex, and the man obviously loves you, but you still have sexual insecurities. She will have those same insecurities, only she will question whether her body is still normal. Again, though, I ask, what is normal? Everyone handles trauma differently. When the right man comes along, he will make her feel whole again."

She reaches out and squeezes my hand in comfort. Watching her, I can't decide who needs it more, me or her, so I wrap my arms around her and hug her tight.

"Mercy, she hasn't always been a friend to me. In her own time, though, she will give your sister exactly what she needs."

"Thank you," Morgan whispers before we part.

Looking back at the closet, she smiles over to me. "Wanna go shopping tomorrow morning? Or do you have hair and make-up appointments?"

"No appointments. I would love to go shopping since I don't even have a dress."

"WHAT?" she shrieks at me. "No dress! This is a travesty we must address."

We laugh together before finalizing our plans for the next morning.

After going back to the party, Morgan pretty much spends her time either at my side or Ice's. We have a lot in common as we both adjust to life as ol' ladies to our badass bikers.

FIVE

CHAPTER
FIVE

PINCH ME

Tessie

"Are you ready now?" Morgan asks excitedly.

We only went to three shops this morning before we found an absolutely perfect one shoulder, empire waist, off-white sun dress. The layers of fabric below my breasts flow freely around and behind me slightly. The one shoulder strap is done to look like roses with one big flower where the strap joins to the top of the dress. My not so large breasts are scooped up by the built in bra, giving me a hint of cleavage I don't normally have. The dress is not over-the-top; it is simple elegance, much like me.

The hotel receptionist made a few calls for us and set up a nice spot on the beach for our vows to take place. She also found a local minister to perform the ceremony on such short notice.

Rex is actually being thoughtful and agreed to rent a car at the airport so none of us had to slow our preparations to pick him and my mom up from the airport. I hope the trip isn't too much on her body.

"I think so," I reply, smiling at Morgan.

"Is it everything you've dreamt of?" she asks, pulling me into a coffee shop.

We order—well, really, she orders—two Cuban espressos as she swears everyone in South Beach is addicted to the ever so small shots of caffeine goodness, while I think on her question. Is this everything I have dreamt of?

"Well, is this your dream come true? If not, what do we need to give you that?"

"Morgan, are you a dreamer? Do you have your wedding planned out along with your version of Prince Charming?" I question, wondering if I am the only woman ever to not dream of her wedding day.

She looks at me shyly before dropping her head. She doesn't answer, which makes me more curious.

"I'll be honest with you. Until Shooter, I never thought I would get married. I certainly didn't believe in Prince Charming. I guess you should know since he will be here today. Shooter is not Axel's dad, and Rex is the complete opposite of prince anything."

"Rex, the Hellion? As in, Shooter's brother?" she questions with a surprised gasp.

"Yeah, Rex, Catawba Hellion VP. So more than Shooter's brother; he's Shooter's Vice Pres."

"Do I even want to know?"

"I'm not a barfly, if that's what you're thinking. I was once Rex's barfly; I guess you could say. It's a long and complicated history he and I share. Axel is the best thing to come out of it for both of us. We're still working on the new dynamic of our relationship, but Rex is there for his son. Being with Rex for years without really being with him warped my ideals of marriage and relationships. For a long time, I was waiting for him to wake up and want any kind of future with me. I was willing to accept anything from him. Then Shooter and I kept getting thrown together. Literally, he was tossed into my life by chance circumstance when my car broke down."

"Damsel in distress … the stuff fairy tales are made of." She smiles sweetly at me.

"Our story is far from a fairy tale, but he is my knight. Maybe not in shining armor, but he is my knight that rides in on his horse of steel to save the day; how about that?" We both laugh.

"Well, how do you feel about it? Is there anything else you want or need?"

"Honestly, I have my man and my son, so I just need my momma, and everything will be complete."

"Simple. I like that about you, Tessie."

We finish our coffees then head back to the hotel. Shooter and Axel are in our room when we walk in.

"Hey, baby," he greets before coming over and kissing me breathless.

"Hey, handsome." Will I ever get tired of kissing this man? Doubtful.

"Fred flew in with your mom and Rex," the man who makes my world spin says with a smile. "My parents are driving but left early enough that, although tired, they will get here about an hour before the ceremony."

"If we have to wait for them, we can. I'm sorry I didn't think of all that when I asked for this."

"Baby, I don't give a shit who is here, as long as when we lay down tonight it's as husband and wife."

"I love you, Andy."

"I love you, too." He kisses me again right as there is a knock at the door.

"Thank goodness someone is here to save us from all their kissing. Morgan, I hope you aren't like this, too," Axel says to my new friend as he bounces past us.

"Party is here, so open the door, fuckers," Rex shouts from the other side of the door.

Axel immediately opens the door and runs to hug my mom. Rex enters our room, leaning down to give me a half hug before greeting Shooter in their half hug, man back slap thing. When his eyes land on Morgan, I can't help laughing.

"Hey, girl. What's your name? You know what, we don't need names. I'll call you Angel, because you're sure to be calling me God later tonight."

"If you want to keep your balls, I wouldn't call her anything but Ice's ol' lady," Shooter replies, laughing as Morgan turns red and backs up to the wall.

Obviously, she has never encountered anyone like Drexel 'Rex' Crews.

"Does that shit really work?" Morgan fires back at him once she has a moment to let his words sink in.

Yes, this one has just the fire and attitude needed to be with a biker. I smile at her.

"Worked on her," Rex tosses his thumb over at me.

"Not really. It's me she's marrying, fucker," Shooter chimes in.

"You're the better man, brother." Rex looks at me seriously. "She deserves nothing but the best."

Tears pool in my eyes. I don't have the same feelings for Rex that I once did. That ship has truly sailed. However, there is a piece of me that will belong to him because he gave me Axel. There really is a heart inside that man. He just doesn't know how to show it or doesn't want to. I haven't figured out which it is yet.

"Rex," I whisper.

"Tessie, I did you wrong. I'm man enough to own that shit. I'm also man enough to stand at this fucker's side when he claims you for eternity. You'll possibly always be the best thing that I ever had, but he was made for you."

"The best is yet to come, Rex," Shooter states, looking to his brother.

"You're standing at his side?" I ask, wondering what these two are conspiring.

"He's family. We're a weird but functional unit. I asked him to be my best man."

Rolling up on my tiptoes, I pull Shooter's head down to kiss him. "I love you, Andy."

"I think I'm gonna be sick from all the feels in this room." Rex grabs at his stomach dramatically. "It's too much emotion for my small heart to take."

"Shut the hell up. Let's go, brother," Shooter says, releasing me.

"Go where?" I ask curiously.

"Guy stuff, Momma. You wouldn't understand," Axel chimes in, taking both Shooter and Rex by the hands and dragging them to the door. "See ya later, Gigi. Love you," he adds, making his way out the door.

Shooter glances over his shoulder at me as he exits and mouths, 'I love you,' before filing out the door behind my little man and my ex.

SIX

CHAPTER SIX

A MOTHER'S LOVE

Morgan leaves not long after the boys so she can get ready. I think I have a new friend in her that will last a long time.

"Momma, want me to curl your hair?"

Tears glisten in her eyes. "I would love that."

When Momma first got sick, it would really upset her that she struggled to wash and brush her own hair. There is a bond we share, not because she is my mom, but because we have been there for each other at our lowest.

When I first came home after the attack, even though I tried to hide my problems, there were nights she would come to my room and just run her fingers through my hair in silent reassurance that I wasn't alone. When I was a little girl, she would do the same thing to put me to sleep after a bad dream.

"Did the trip take too much out of you, Momma?"

"Rex was good about helping me maneuver around, and I used my wheelchair in the airports, so I wasn't walking too far." She wipes her eyes as she settles in on the hotel toilet seat while I plug in the curling iron. "Tessie, I'm proud of you."

"Momma—"

"Let me finish. Things haven't been easy for us."

I run my fingers through her hair to get the tangles out. "Me and you always." Picking up the brush, I separate her hair into a section, apply some holding spray, and begin to curl her hair.

"Shooter is an answer to my prayers."

"Momma—" I start as I see the tears roll down her cheeks.

"Tessie, there will come a time when I won't be here. Until Shooter, I was worried about you. I tried to teach you, to guide you, but I got sick. Because of that, I haven't always been the mom I wanted to be. I've prayed for you to have what I didn't have, for Axel to have what I didn't give you. Shooter does that. He puts my heart at ease for you. Tessie, you are my world."

Tears freely run down my cheeks as I release the curl and set the hot iron down.

"Momma—" I try to choke out.

"He is my every wish for you. He is my answered prayer. You were my gift at the end of every day, baby girl. Axel, he's a gift to you. But, honey, you deserve so much more and that is Shooter. He's good, baby girl. He's never gonna leave you or Axel. He's solid. He is a real man. All of that is there with Shooter. Today, when you take those vows along with his name, you are getting something good, baby girl. You will be the only woman he will ever love. He will give you his name, his love, and his everything. He will take care of you. He will give you the best of him. Your burdens will be carried by him, no longer on your own. Tessie, he will lay the world at your feet and fight with everything inside him to ease your struggles. He will make the days come easy and make the moments last. He is your light. He is your gift at the end of every day."

With shaking hands, I go about another curl as we both let the tears freely fall. Everything she says about Shooter is true—they don't come any better than the man I am marrying today.

"I know, Momma, and I love him for it." I release

another curl and go about the next one.

"And he does you, as well. Today, I will proudly watch you become a wife to a truly honorable man. Today, I can breathe easier because, when I am no more, Shooter will be there to hold your hand. As a mom, I worry for you. I wonder who will be there for you when the day ends. Since you found Shooter, I don't worry anymore. He will always take care of your every need. He will be your rock."

"You've always been my rock, Momma," I reply, not wanting her to feel replaced.

"And you are my rock, Tessie. You are my very best friend, you are my safe place, and you are my world. You are more than my daughter. You always have been. You're my reason for being."

I wipe the tears from my face as I try to move onto the next curl.

"As the saying goes, today, Shooter 'takes' you as his wife. Even though things will change, I'm not losing my daughter; I'm gaining a son. Enjoy your day, baby girl. This is the first day of the rest of your life."

While her words sink in, I release the curl, setting the curling iron on the countertop. Without a word, I wrap my arms around her. I love Shooter with every breath I take. I am completely confident in marrying him, but something about having this moment with my mom makes it feel so right and so real.

CHAPTER SEVEN

BEYOND A LIFETIME

SHOOTER

"Jeans, man. I think we should wear jeans. Tessie said simple," Rex whines.

"Suck it up. Tessie wants simple, but I want her mom to know we do clean up all right."

We went out and bought white button up shirts and khaki pants for tonight. The ceremony is on the beach, so we are all going barefoot. No ties, nothing fancy, but my woman deserves to see her little man dressed up as he walks her down the aisle to me. If Axel is dressing up, Rex and I will, too. Well, our version of it.

"My dick feels restrained in these pants."

"Shut the hell up," I laugh at my brother.

After we finish helping Axel spike his hair, we make our way down to the beach. I give hellos to Fred and my parents as they settle into the white folding chairs that have been set out for everyone. Pride swells in me as I take in the people who have surprised us by showing up.

Rex did his own thing to make sure all the important people share this moment with us. Roundman, Danza, Tank, Sass, Frisco, and even Amy from the Haywood's Landing charter are here. Tripp, Doll, Boomer—with Purple Pussy Pamela on his arm—and even Caroline are here from Catawba. Bowie, Lock, and Shay are in attendance since they were still in town from the graduation, and Ice and his crew are all settled in.

Family.

In one way or another, these people are all family to Tessie and me.

Rex escorts her mom down to her seat slowly and carefully. Taking a moment, I make my way over to her.

"Rex, take Axel to his mom so he can escort her down please." He smiles at me as I kneel in front of my soon-to-be mother-in-law's chair.

"I promise you, here and now, to take care of your daughter, her son, our children, and you. Today, as I stand up there, I not only commit my life to Tessie, but to you and Axel."

Tears fill her eyes as she simply nods at me.

I squeeze her hand as I stand back up and take my place to wait for my bride. Blowing out a breath, I drop my head to my feet to take in this moment. When we leave here today, she will be my wife and I her husband. Something I never thought I would have is happening today.

When I look up, she takes my breath away. At the end of the make-shift aisle is my very reason for being —my son and my bride. He may be Rex's by blood, but in my heart, he is just as much mine.

When her eyes meet mine, I have to remind myself to inhale. Never has she looked so beautiful. It is not the dress or her hair, although they are gorgeous; it is every-thing that is Tessie. Nothing is over-done, because she doesn't need all that. Her beauty comes from the heart and radiates out into everyone and everything around her.

They reach the end of the aisle, our boy practically bouncing in excitement. He looks up at me, smiling bigger than ever before.

"She's beautiful, isn't she, Shooter?" Axel asks me.

Before I can reply, Rex is stepping from behind me to high-five our son.

"Hell yes, she is, little man. You made an awesome escort. Looking good, buddy," Rex whispers to Axel. I don't know if I want to smack him for looking at my woman or laugh for the real bond he shares now with his son.

"Yeah, Axel, she's the most beautiful girl in the whole world," I say, not taking my eyes off my bride.

"Duh, she's mom. You always say that, but today she's rockin'," Axel says with so much enthusiasm none of us can keep from laughing.

The officiant clears his throat to begin the ceremony. We have met with him briefly, giving him an idea of who we are and what we are about. We decided to give him time to open the ceremony a little bit, then we will share in our personal vows before closing out. Since this was not planned, we didn't bring our rings, and our ceremony will be far from traditional, much like everything else about us.

As he begins his opening words, my chest swells with emotions. "Today, there will be no dearly beloved, no ancient rhyme of the married. Today, there are no dead languages to solemnize vows that are very much alive and will remain so for a lifetime. Today, promises become permanent. Two friends join together in love to become family. Today is not about the words spoken or the rings exchanged. It is not about grand pronouncements and recessional marches.

"This day is the day Andy and Tessie share their love with all of you as they commit to one another for this lifetime and beyond. For love knows no boundaries between this life and eternity. The love they share is one that it is all-encompassing. The love they share is one that is consuming, one that is as necessary as your next breath."

When Tessie's eyes fill with tears, I want to reach out and hold her, but it is not time yet. The words he speaks are so true, making me want nothing more than to hold her close now and always.

The officiant continues, "However, love isn't simply a word; it's an action. Love isn't something you say; it's something you do. Love is genuine, honest, and open. Love is compassionate, kind, passionate, and blind. Love doesn't know space or time. As the Bible says in Corinthians, *'Love bears all things, believes all things, hopes all things, and endures all things.'*

"Not only do Tessie and Andy love one another romantically—it's in every look, every touch, and every moment they're together—they also share the love of friendship. That love and enjoyment of each other in friendship will help sustain the promises they make today. Everyone here will help solidify this bond. This new journey will be at times richly rewarding and other times extremely difficult. Most importantly, this will be a ride you take together. With that, we will begin.

"Who gives this woman to be married to this man?"

Axel makes a face before reaching out to me. I squat down in front of him, concerned about his reaction.

"Shooter, I can't give her to you. This wasn't part of the deal. You said hold her hand and bring her down the aisle to you. I mean, we can like share her, but I can't give her to you. She's my mom."

I almost fall back laughing. Tessie is squeezing his hand and laughing as are everyone that could hear him. God, I love this little boy.

"We're gonna share her. I'm not takin' your mom away, I promise."

Axel looks up to the officiant innocently. "We're gonna share her. So I can't say I'm giving her to anyone. Can she still get married, mister?"

The officiant laughs before replying, "Well, as long as no one objects, yes, son, she can still get married." He looks out to our guests. "Is there anyone with any reason that these two should not join together as husband and wife today? Speak now, or forever hold your peace."

When the moment passes and no one objects, he nods down to Axel. "Looks like we have a wedding to finish. How about you let Andy hold your mom's hands and you come stand here with me?"

Axel does just that.

Once Tessie's hands are in mine, I feel her squeeze. In this moment, my heart feels so full it may just burst.

"I love you," I whisper to her as her eyes glisten with unshed tears.

The officiant begins, "Marriage is much more than your signatures on a legal contract. Today, you will make promises to each other in front of all these people that you love. Today, you are giving your word, your lives, and your love to one another for eternity. No pastor or priest or justice of the peace can create a marriage, because a marriage truly is nothing except the promises made and kept by two individuals. Andy and Tessie, your wedding day is one brief day in time. Although your vows are spoken in a matter of minutes, they are promises that will last a lifetime."

Tessie smiles sweetly at me, knowing that for both of us this truly is the beginning of our future. A happiness neither of us imagined possible has been gifted to us in what has been a hard ride through life.

"Will you, Andy, cherish Tessie as your lawfully wedded wife, protecting her, tending to her needs through illness, disappointment, and all of life's challenges?"

"With all that I have and all that I will be, I will," I answer honestly, proudly, and with more love than I have ever felt in my lifetime.

"Will you strive to understand her, giving her comfort when she seeks it from you? Will you try never to say in anger that which you wouldn't say in friendship? When night falls, will you go to sleep with thanks for her presence at your side and renewed love for her in your heart?"

"I will for eternity."

He turns his attention to Tessie.

"Will you, Tessie, cherish Andy as your lawfully wedded husband, protecting him, tending to his needs through illness, disappointment, and all of life's challenges?"

"I will," she replies as she smiles at me.

"Will you strive to understand him, giving him comfort when he seeks it from you? Will you try never to say in anger that which you wouldn't say in friendship? When night falls, will you sleep with thanks for his presence at your side and renewed love for him in your heart?"

"I will for eternity."

I want to kiss her. I want to hold her to me. I want to take her home and show her just how much I love her. Forget the guests and ceremony. I am bursting with love for this woman, and I want nothing more than to join together as one with her body as much as we are joining our lives together right now.

The officiant looks to me, opening the time for us to recite the vows we have chosen to write ourselves.

As a tear falls from her face, I reach up to wipe it away with my thumb. She lays her face gently into my hand, and I lose all of my thoughts.

"Tessie, baby, I love you. I honor you. I cherish you. I promise to love you more tomorrow than I do today. I promise to honor you for always in all ways. I promise to cherish you, not only for the woman you are, but the woman you once were and the woman you will become as time changes. I promise to endure all things with you.

"It hasn't always been easy for us apart, and it won't always be easy for us together, but I promise you won't be alone. I promise I will be your strength when you have none. I promise to be your shelter when the storms rage on. I promise to give you the best of myself and ask no more of you than you can give. I promise to accept you exactly as you are. I love you for the woman you are and the woman you have yet to become. I promise to be open to you. I promise to grow alongside you. I promise to be willing to face life as we both change in order to keep our relationship alive and thriving."

I bring both my hands up to cup her face, wiping more tears with my thumbs as she stares into my eyes and straight to my soul. I want so badly to kiss her, but I know I have to wait. "I promise to love you in good times and in bad, with all I have to give and in the only way I know how … completely. It's you and me, baby, for eternity."

With shaking hands, she reaches up and holds my wrists as I continue to cup her face and wipe her tears. It may not be effective, but I need this connection to her, and not just holding her hands.

"Andy. Where do I begin? I love you. I honor you. I cherish you. I promise to love you more tomorrow than I do today. I promise to honor you for always, in all ways. I promise to cherish you, not only for the man you are, but the man you once were, and the man you will become as time changes. I promise to lean on you in times of trouble and in times of celebration. I promise to endure all things with you. I promise to give you the very best of myself and ask no more of you than you can give. I promise to accept you exactly as you are. I promise to hold on tight when the ride isn't smooth. I promise to cherish you, your cars, and your Harley." We all laugh as my woman lightens the mood.

"I promise not to shut you out. I promise to let you inside to my fears, feelings, secrets, and dreams. I promise to grow alongside you. I promise to be willing to face life as we both change in order to keep our relationship alive and thriving." She grips my wrists tighter and blows out a breath. "I promise to love you in good times and in bad, with all I have to give and in the only way I know how … completely. It's you and me, baby, for eternity."

As we conclude our vows, the officiant adds, "You are promising in front of all of these witnesses that you want to be with each other and only each other for the rest of your lives. You are committing to do everything in your power to honor the promises you are making here today."

I slide my hands down to link behind the back of Tessie's neck, rubbing her jawline with my thumbs.

"Since our couple has chosen not to exchange rings today, it is with great honor that I now pronounce you husband and wife. You may kiss your bride."

And kiss her I do.

EIGHT

RIDE ON

"You want to do what?" I ask Shooter.

"Let's all go to Disney World for the honeymoon." He is completely serious, and I think he may be insane.

"Have you lost your fuckin' mind? You just married the woman of your dreams, and you want to go to Disney World! Asshole, take your woman to an island and fuck her until she doesn't know her name. That's why women take their man's name—if you fuck 'em right, they can't remember."

I laugh at him. "Shut the hell up, Rex."

"Seriously, take Tessie some place nice, just the two of you. I'll take Axel and Gigi home and handle them until you return."

"Man, haven't you heard the saying 'happy wifey, happy lifey'? Wifey wants to take her son to Disney. She wants your ass there so neither of you miss his first trip to the land of magic. Bottom line, Tessie doesn't ask me for much. She wants this; she gets this. So we're gonna suck it up and go."

"Think of the pictures, Rex. You and Shooter in your Hellion cuts and mouse ears!" Tessie laughs from behind him.

"No fuckin' way. I'll go on this little adventure if this is what you really want, but no way, no how am I wearing some damn mouse ears." I put my hands on my hips, trying to look firm in my resolve.

"We'll see about that." Tessie smirks at me.

"You really want me to go on your honeymoon? I think there is something seriously wrong with our family dynamic," I question honestly.

"I want to do something that includes Axel. I don't want him to think he's losing me. If Shooter and I go off on a honeymoon, then he loses me on only day two for how many days? I was a mom before I became his wife, and Axel has enough change right now."

"Woman, you aren't mine, never were met to be, but damn you are the best mom for our kid. Thank you, Tessie, seriously."

My ex-lover blushes at me. There was a time when making her blush was the highlight of my lonely days. The life I lead is not one made for a family. Never really thought about a future and having someone by my side until Tessie was attacked. Then, finding out about Axel... Well, it rocked my world at first. Now, I can't imagine life without the little hell raiser.

I have two weeks free before Tripp has me going away for a negotiation. I guess the first week will be spent with mouse ears. Maybe I can find a princess to fuck my time away with. I would rather be balls deep in 'Lux,' but she has to get back to work. It doesn't help that she refuses to give me the time of day. She only challenges me to want her more. *Fight it, baby*. I am not afraid of working for my rewards. In the meantime, a man has needs, ones I need filled.

Having her here for the wedding was the first break she has taken in the last few months. According to her, she has taken on two new clients, trying to move her way up to a head accounting position so she doesn't have to continue to be an assistant. Yeah, an assistant to the asshole causing her trouble, but she left that part out. Her naivety is going to get her in a bad situation. The douche she works for is not going to back off just because she gets a different position. No, that sick fucker will only start imagining more compromising positions he plans to have her in.

The thing she needs to learn about the Hellions is that you can't ask us for help in a moment of panic and then turn us away. We protect what is ours. Like a dog with a bone, we don't let go. Tripp and I know too much now. She needs me more than she realizes, but she keeps refusing my help. I wish she would understand my lifestyle, my club and my family. She needs to learn that, with the Hellions, we are along for the ride, no matter how dangerous, bumpy, or long.

My dick twitches thinking of her. The ride with her may just be the challenge of my life. The ride for her may just be exactly what I need.

Things are a little clearer for me now. Change doesn't happen overnight, but it does happen. I will take this week with my son; however, when I get home, things are changing for me and for her situation. She once asked me if my intentions in helping her were innocent.

Lux, there is nothing innocent about the ride I plan to take you on.

~The End~
Until the next ride…

NOTES

Desert Ghosts MC used with permission from author Theresa Marguerite Hewitt, Ricochet, book 1 of the Desert Ghosts MC series coming soon.

Savage Outlaws MC used with permission from author Emily Minton. Beautiful Outlaw, book 1 of the Savage Outlaw MC series is available now!!!

Keep reading for an excerpt from Innocent Ride, Hellions Ride Book 5 – available through all major ebook retailers.

INNOCENT RIDE EXCERPT

Innocent Ride

Opposites really do attract.

She is a corporate accountant. Her life is full of structure, routine, and organization. Caroline Milton loves knowing what to expect every minute of every day. More importantly, she knows her life is in her control, which is not at all what she came from.

When a situation spirals out of control at work, Caroline turns to the one group she least expected to find herself dependent on—the Hellions motorcycle club.

He is the Catawba Hellions VP, and a wild one who refuses to be tamed. Where women are concerned, Drexel "Rex" Crews lives by the motto: "hit it, get it, and go; no repeats." His life suddenly tilts on its axis when his wild days come barreling back with major responsibilities.

Rex finally has a real reason to settle down.

Asked as a personal favor from Doll to protect her best friend, Rex can't refuse.

Protecting Caroline was supposed to be an innocent task. However, the attraction from their first meeting is a fire burning strong inside them both. Neither can deny the pull, despite them coming from different worlds.

Can this innocent ride turn into a long-lasting love?

THE MAN I AM

REX

As the wind whips around me, she dances violently, slapping the leather of my cut harshly against my T-shirt covered chest. A storm is brewing in the air around me as another one rages on inside my darkened soul.

The road before me is curvy. They call it Dead Man's Trail. Riding a ledge is what it feels like. With the fine line of one wrong move, life and death are in the balance as the road winds through a mountain.

I am hours from home, and I still can't bring myself to turn around and go back. I am not on a transport or on a run for the club. I am out alone, just me, my Harley, and the open night sky.

Not a star shines tonight as the humidity rises and the wind swirls through the thick air. A summer storm is in the midst. My mind races as the pipes on my bike scream out under the pressure of my speed.

"Be a man to be proud of. Carry your name—our name—with pride," Pop's voice echoes in my head.

A name. My name. Our name.

Tessie gave my boy—her son, my son, our son—my name. *My* fucking name.

Axel Devon Crews. Mini-me. One look and I fucking knew he was mine. My gut twists. *Mine.* My blood. My responsibility. My name. My fucking mirror image.

Throttle down, I push on faster, harder, needing to feel something slice through me besides the disappointments running through my mind. My life is officially at a crossroads, every mistake of my past now shoved in the forefront of my mind.

How did I get so lost? How have I become so consumed in things that don't matter? When did I become so self-absorbed?

I would lay down my life to protect the very cut moving across my back right now. Yet, the woman who freely lay beneath me, giving her body, heart, and soul to me, I left without a glance back. She ripped her body —literally—to give life to my seed, and I did nothing more than wink, smile, and move on to the next woman. I was so focused on myself I missed the signs. I should have known. Hell, I should have been there.

Then, when the opportunity came for me to step up for her, did I do it? No. Shooter stepped in like I knew he would. He is a far better man than I am. Tessie deserves a man like him, not the mess that is me. No matter what life throws at them, he will be there to have her back, to be her security. He will be her strength and her calm within the storm. He will be her best friend and her lover. Everything that Tessie needs, wants, and damn sure deserves is found in the man I now proudly call my brother.

Sure, there was a time I wanted to rip him limb from limb. He went after what could have been mine. No, he didn't go after her, not really, not if I keep it real with myself. I pushed him there. I sent him to her. I gave him what could have been my future. The only person to blame here is me. She needed me, and I tossed her off to him. My mistakes. My losses. I know, if I am ever given a chance to have something good again, I am not going to waste my opportunity.

When the clouds open up, the hot rain comes down, pelting me in the face, on my arms, and all my exposed skin. The road beneath me gets slick as I push on. Soft gravel gives way, and my back tire shifts under me. I don't correct the movement. The delicate balance keeping me upright drops as does my bike, and my body hits the pavement hard. Gravel digs in even through the denim of my pants as the material rips. I feel my arms shred as my bike is no longer under my now broken body, only the unforgiving road.

Broken, shredded, a bloody mess of a man—that is what I am.

Pops' voice is the last thing to sound through my head as I succumb to the blackness consuming me.

"The past is the past; the future is before you. Change is a power we all hold. Learning from your mistakes is growth, and it's a necessary change. How you pick yourself up when you hit rock bottom will tell what kind of man you really are."

INNOCENT RIDE

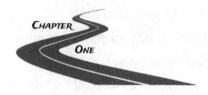

CHAPTER ONE

NIGHTMARES

Caroline

"You said yes."

"To dinner as friends," I reply harshly.

"Come on, you can't be that naïve. You want this as much as I do. Give into it. No need to deny either of us."

"Chad, I don't feel this is appropriate, since we work together." *And, since I think you are a complete douche, we really shouldn't do this.* I get the distinct feeling now is not the time for me to share this with him, though.

"No one will know. Work is irrelevant unless you

plan on telling someone." He has his hands on my waist, making my skin crawl. "You can't deny me. You won't deny me. You've made yourself available to me for months now."

"What?" I shriek in disbelief. "Are you delusional? It was all for my job, not for you."

He runs his hands up and down my arms, sending a cold chill down my spine.

"I'll make you feel so good," Chad says seductively as he pulls me to him. His erection presses against my belly, making me want to vomit.

I shake my head back and forth. *No. No. No.*

He has the wrong idea. This was supposed to be a celebratory dinner after securing my first new client.

His hands move up to my neck. As they close in on my throat painfully, adrenaline kicks in. In fight or flight mode, tears prick behind my now closed eyelids while his lips crash down on mine as he squeezes my windpipe.

The pressure to breathe builds. The helpless feeling engulfs me. Panic sets in. He is choking me firmly as he sucks harshly on my bottom lip before biting down. I am numb in fear as I taste the metallic flavor of my own blood.

Beep.

Beep.

Beep.

My alarm blaring brings me out of my slumber. I am, yet again, drenched in sweat as I rouse from my nightmare. Shaking off the negative thoughts, I look around me. The soft grays and lavenders of my very girlie bedroom come into clear vision slowly. My grandmother's rocker sits by my window for reading, unmoving, as I remind myself I am safe. The delicate swirls of color beam off my Tiffany style lamp on my night stand as the blinking of my alarm clock seems to bring my world to life.

"He didn't get me," I whisper to the air around me.

A knee to his groin and an elbow to the back of his head as he hunched down from the first impact secured my small window of time to run.

And run I did, straight to my car, and then I drove to Delilah's house. That was my second mistake. My first being to ever put myself in the situation I was in with the likes of Chad the scumbag.

In my panic, I couldn't think of anyone or anywhere safer than Delilah 'Doll' Reklinger, now Crews, and her Hellions MC family.

She put me up at her place for a few days until I could make some decisions and sort my life out. Afterward, facing my fears, my insecurities, and my mess of a life, I picked up the pieces and went back to work, realizing I could handle the ass-hat on my own —well, sort of. All in all, I have it under control in my own way, and I was hoping Doll would drop it. Wrong.

Some things are better left alone. Too bad she disagrees with me in this situation.

Worse than that, her man, Tripp, got involved. Then Tripp's cousin, Rex, joined the pity Caroline party that wants to feel sorry for me; the party that wants to simply fix what I created. I did this. It is completely my fault. Why don't they stop feeling sorry for me and see this is a product of my own stupidity?

Rex refuses to understand my stance on remaining quiet. Yes, my college best friend, Delilah, got her man and his band of bikers to swoop in and put a watch on me, a watch that one Drexel 'Rex' Crews has decided to make his personal mission to handle.

Rex doesn't even know what happened; Delilah has kept my secret safe about that night. She only reached out to tell them that I was having problems with a guy at work. I shouldn't have put myself out there. Rex doesn't want to hear any of this, though. He is hell bent and heaven sent on finding out every little detail. Why can't he let a sleeping dog lie?

Climbing out of my bed, I immediately start stripping my sweat-soaked sheets. Ugh, this is getting old.

All those years of school, all the focus and dedication I used to graduate at the top of my program, wasted.

While Delilah and Savannah enjoyed our college years, I tucked myself away studying over laws and numbers.

All for what?

To end up a two bit whore to my supervisor? Fuck that! Women have worked for decades before me to secure a place for the female sex in employment. Women have sacrificed money, time, and having families of their own to pave their way in so many male-dominated industries, such as corporate accounting. The mountain may be high to climb, but I refuse to give up just because some male chauvinist pig feels my only place is under him in business, in bed, or both. I am blessed to have this job, and I refuse to give it up easily, even if it is a battle of wills to get up and make my way in every single day.

Kenna, a friend of a friend of Delilah's and the Hellions motorcycle club, actually secured the junior position for me. Since we didn't truly know each other, I feel confident that I got the job on my own merit. She merely opened the door by putting her name out there to get the interview for me, so when it came time for assignments, she didn't feel comfortable being my direct supervisor. Favoritism and all that, I get it.

This left me with Chad, the devil's spawn, himself. Chad, my head accountant, my lead, my direct supervisor. Also, the man who has pushed every boundary there is and made sure to set it up so it could be portrayed as my doing. Chad, the master manipulator. Chad, the scumbag. Chad, my boss who I have to face every single day, including today.

I am not powerless. I am not powerless. I can do this yet again; I continue repeating in my head as my new morning mantra. I have to remind myself I got away, remind myself I have the power to push through this and so much more. He will not win. He will not run me off. I will stand strong. I will move on, one foot in front of the other, one step at a time, one day at a time.

Never the lesser, never be weak, rise above, and power through.

Time heals all wounds, or so they say.

I may have physically healed from crashing my bike, but mentally, I am far from it. I know someone was watching over me that night. To walk away from a crash like that with only road rash is a miracle.

Too bad I can't say my bike fared so well. It resembles my life: pieces hanging by a wire, unrecognizable paint, and only running by sheer force.

When I look in the mirror, I don't know the man staring back at me. I am going through the motions by mere willpower to do better tomorrow than I do today and did yesterday.

I failed him.

I failed my son.

I failed his mother.

I failed Pops.

I failed myself.

I failed, period, end of story.

With the road laid before me, I took the wrong path. I guess, in some ways, I have always been on the wrong path. Pops taught me better than that. Did I listen, though? Fuck no.

Tripp and I have always been rebels, until Roundman came along and gave us a different direction. Beyond my brotherhood in the Hellions, my world is all about me, always has been. What I want, when I want it, and how the fuck I want it.

I slap my hand down on the bar to let Corinne know I need another beer, and she immediately uncaps and sets the ice cold brew in front of me. Corinne is cute enough; a short little thing with tits and hips. She has sucked me off before in the stockroom here at Ruthless ... the stockroom that I can't go back into without rage overtaking me. Just thinking of that room and what happened to Tessie, my blood boils.

Sensing something is off with me, Corinne rounds the bar and stands beside me. She is in a short denim skirt, a tight as fuck black halter top, and black heels—optimum clothing for prime tips.

"Rex," she says huskily, the tips of her nipples poking out the fabric of her shirt, making it known she isn't wearing a bra.

I don't reply immediately; I run my hand around the back of her leg, up her thigh, to the sweet juncture between them. As I suspected, no panties, either.

I barely dip my fingertip in the wetness of her core. Circling the edge of her cunt, I tease her as her juices build on my fingertip. Her breath hitches and she moves closer to me.

"So wet, you dirty girl. Were you thinkin' of me all day? Were you waitin' for me to come here today and pet this little pussy of yours?" I rub my fingers through her folds and over her clit as she moans in need.

"Yes, Rex. My pussy wants all your attention." Corrine pushes herself onto my hand more.

I shake my head as I remove my hand and stand. Then, nodding to Purple Pussy Pamela so she knows she is on her own for the next few minutes, I guide Corinne to the back pool room.

She turns around to face me, and I wrap my large hands around her neck as her eyes get big, and her pulse races. I don't apply pressure, but my hands are in a spot that I know makes her feel vulnerable. I also know she gets off on this.

When she licks her lips in need and want, I release her neck and turn her around. She is short. Add my height to the mix, and she barely makes it to my pecs.

Positioning her facing the wall lined with chairs and dartboards, I lift one of her legs, bending her knee and setting that sky high, fuck me heel on the edge of the chair. Pushing her skirt up, I expose her ass, and she arches, giving me even more.

Unbuttoning my jeans, I then unzip them enough to release the beast that is my cock. Grabbing a condom from my wallet, I sheath myself carefully, avoiding any possible tears on the condom from my piercing.

Corinne turns her head to look over her shoulder at me. Tugging roughly on her hair, I twist her head sideways and push her into the wall. Without warning, I use my other hand to spread her ass cheeks and slam my rock hard cock in her dripping pussy. Oh, yeah, the girl likes it rough, and that is how she is going to get it, too.

Her mouth drops open to make an 'O' as I pound away relentlessly. Forgetting everything and everyone around us, I slide in and out of her heat, taking my frustrations out as I squish her face into the wall. Her head slides up as I slide in balls deep, and she hits the bottom of the dart board, causing it to fall off the wall and hits my arm, as well as her back, on its way down. She tries to reach out to grab it, but I only pull her hair harder, causing her to put her hands back on the wall to seek relief. The dart board crashes to the floor with a thud. I pound away.

Her head hits the wall as I continue my unforgiving rhythm. Her pussy clinches me, milking my cock. Her body is begging for release. She is on the edge; I feel it as she tenses further with each thrust. Oh, yeah, she is right there. I almost laugh when she moans loudly.

She moves one of her hands off the wall to touch her clit. She wants it. She wants that high. The build-up. The anticipation. The games we as males and females play. The tease. The seductive dance of getting off. She is so close I can taste it in the air around us. Normally, getting a girl off would feed my ego. Any other time, I would push her hand away and be the one to send her over the edge.

Thinking of going over the edge, I feel my balls tighten. The tingle climbs my spine, and I slam into her harshly one last time, releasing my seed into the condom between us.

She rocks back into my softening cock, seeking her own orgasm. Any other time, I would have held back on my release to give her hers first since she was right there. Suddenly, though, I feel sick and pull out of her.

As I let go of her head, she looks at me and pouts.

Fucking pouts.

I shake my head as I remove the condom, tying off the top before tossing it in the trashcan in the corner.

Corinne is taking her foot down when I reach out and pull her to me. Using the bottom of her shirt, I wipe my dick off before putting it in my jeans.

A fire of pure, contained fury dances in her eyes. She is pissed, rightfully so.

"I was so close, and you just stopped, fucker."

"Yeah, I did," I reply arrogantly.

"You really wiped your cock off on my shirt?"

"Yeah, I did. Watch yourself, Corinne; you're testing the waters. Keep treading the way you are, and you're gonna drown."

"Fuck you, Rex." She huffs, pulling her skirt down and trying to gauge the damage of the stains of my cum on her shirt.

"Know your place, Corinne. This is the only warning you'll get from me, and you're lucky I'm givin' you that."

Buttoning my jeans, I feel my phone vibrate in my back pocket. Rather than continue to give any more of my attention to Corinne, I turn and walk out of the bar without a second look back as I take my phone out of my pocket.

As I step outside, the fresh air assaults my nose. The bar is always smoke-filled, and the night air is a welcomed reprieve to my lungs.

"Yo," I answer my phone, knowing it is Tripp.

"Got a nine-one-oh. Meet me at the office in ten."

He disconnects the call that just informed me that I have a club run to handle. Great. My head is so not in this. Push on, though, because that is the name of my game, for now.

This story continues on in Innocent Ride (Hellions Ride 5)

NOTE FROM CHELSEA

Thank you for taking a ride with the Hellions MC in *Eternal Ride*! For those of you who have NOT read the Hellions Ride Series, I bet you're pretty confused right about now. The thing is, this is a short story that is meant to be read after *Merciless Ride*. If you liked the characters in this short story, and would like to learn more about them, please feel free to check out the Hellions Ride Series.

The Hellions Ride Series reading order is One Ride, Forever Ride, Merciless Ride, Eternal Ride, and coming next Innocent Ride. Merciless Ride can be read as a stand-alone novel, however, the characters are first introduced in One Ride and reading it will build up your suspense level a little more should you choose to read them in order.

Others who have read the Hellions Ride Series

might be wondering, "When's the next book?" *Innocent Ride*, featuring Drexel 'Rex' Crews, is now available so pick up your copy today and take a ride with Rex and Lux.

I hope you enjoyed reading this book as much as I enjoyed writing it. If you did, please consider leaving a review at your favorite online retailers, such as Amazon and Barnes & Noble, or review websites such as Goodreads. These are great ways to help spread the word about books to readers who have yet to discover them. There are excerpts from my friends' books, so make sure you keep turning those pages! Happy reading!

ABOUT THE AUTHOR

USA Today and *Wall Street Journal* bestselling author Chelsea Camaron is a small-town Carolina girl with a big imagination. She's a wife and mom, chasing her dreams. She writes contemporary romance, romantic suspense, and romance thrillers. She loves to write about blue-collar men who have real problems with a fictional twist. From mechanics, bikers, oil riggers, smokejumpers, bar owners, and beyond she loves a strong hero who works hard and plays harder.

Chelsea can be found on social media at:
    Facebook: www.facebook.com/authorchelseacamaron
    Twitter: @chelseacamaron
    Instagram: @chelseacamaron
    Website: www.authorchelseacamaron.com
    Email chelseacamaron@gmail.com
    Join Chelsea's reader group here: http://bit.ly/2BzvTa4

ALSO BY CHELSEA CAMARON

Love and Repair Series:

Crash and Burn

Restore My Heart

Salvaged

Full Throttle

Beyond Repair

Stalled

Box Set Available

Hellions Ride Series:

One Ride

Forever Ride

Merciless Ride

Eternal Ride

Innocent Ride

Simple Ride

Heated Ride

Ride with Me (Hellions MC and Ravage MC Duel with Ryan Michele)

Originals Ride

Final Ride

Hellions Ride On Series:

Hellions Ride On Prequel

Born to It

Bastard in It

Bleed for It

Breathe for It

Bold from It

Broken by It

Brazen being It

Better as It

Blue Collar Bad Boys Series:

Maverick

Heath

Lance

Wendol

Reese

Devil's Due MC Series:

Serving My Soldier

Crossover

In The Red

Below The Line

Close The Tab

Day of Reckoning

Paid in Full

Bottom Line

Almanza Crime Family Duet

Cartel Bitch

Cartel Queen

Romantic Thriller Series:

Stay

Seeking Solace: Angelina's Restoration

Reclaiming Me: Fallyn's Revenge

Bad Boys of the Road Series:

Mother Trucker

Panty Snatcher

Azzhat

Santa, Bring Me a Biker!

Santa, Bring Me a Baby!

Stand Alone Reads:

Romance – Moments in Time Anthology

Shenanigans (Currently found in the Beer Goggles Anthology

She is …

The following series are co-written

The Fire Inside Series:

(co-written by Theresa Marguerite Hewitt)

Kale

Regulators MC Series:

(co-written by Jessie Lane)

Ice

Hammer

Coal

Summer of Sin Series:

(co-written with Ripp Baker, Daryl Banner, Angelica Chase,
MJ Fields, MX King)

Original Sin

Caldwell Brothers Series:

(co-written by USA Today Bestselling Author MJ Fields)

Hendrix

Morrison

<u>Jagger</u>

Stand Alone Romance:

(co-written with USA Today Bestselling Author MJ Fields)

<u>Visibly Broken</u>

<u>Use Me</u>

Ruthless Rebels MC Series:

(co-written with Ryan Michele)

<u>Shamed</u>

<u>Scorned</u>

<u>Scarred</u>

<u>Schooled</u>

Box Set Available

Power Chain Series:

(co-written with Ryan Michele)

<u>Power Chain FREE eBook</u>

<u>PowerHouse</u>

<u>Power Player</u>

<u>Powerless</u>

<u>OverPowered</u>

CPSIA information can be obtained
at www.ICGtesting.com
Printed in the USA
LVHW052229080321
680888LV00015B/2523

9 781519 784483